Spontaneously Combustible

Adapted by H. B. Gilmour
From the script by Mark Steen
and Mark Palmer

SCHOLASTIC INC.
New York Toronto London Auckland Sydney

For Jason Weissman and Dorothy Dubrule

Based on the TV series *Aaahh!!! Real Monsters*™ created by Klasky/Csupo Inc. as seen on Nickelodeon®

Cover illustration by Don Cassity
The text of this book was set in Stempel Garamond.
The interior illustrations are from the video,
enhanced in Adobe Photoshop™ by Don Cassity.

ISBN 0-590-35117-6

12 11 10 9 8 7 6 5 4 3 2 1   7 8 9/9 0 1 2/0

Printed in the U.S.A.   40

First Scholastic printing, December 1997

The full moon shone down on the foul-smelling river.

There in the darkness, where rats scurried and bugs crawled, three scary monster friends were fishing.

"What a beautiful night," Oblina said, tossing her hook into the steaming water.

Slender and striped, with spidery eyelashes, Oblina was one of the very best students at the Monster Academy.

"I'm going to catch something really disgusting," ugly, hairy Krumm bragged.

Krumm was not the brightest young monster at school, but he was certainly the smelliest.

Standing between his two best friends, Ickis impatiently jiggled his fishing pole. "I hope I catch something juicy and disgusting," said the purple monster.

Like every monster at the Academy, Ickis wanted to terrify humans.

That was what they all were training for at school.

Something tugged on Oblina's line.

"Got one!" she shouted proudly.

Oblina's flexible body bent forward like a fishing pole as she strained against her catch.

Finally, she whipped herself backward and reeled in a large rubber boot.

It was slimy and grimy, filled with great green globs of muck.

"What a beauty," Krumm said, admiring Oblina's boot.

"Yes, it is," she agreed. Her bright red lips curled in a satisfied grin.

Removing the boot from her hook, Oblina tossed it onto the pile of mashed and mangled treasures she'd already caught.

Now Krumm's line began to bob.

"Hold my eyes!" he shouted excitedly.

Krumm's eyeballs were perfectly round and white.

He handed his eyeballs to Oblina.

Krumm pulled with so much force that the leaky old tire he had hooked flew over his head and landed with a *bump-bump-bump* behind him.

"What is it? What is it?" he asked.

Without his eyeballs, Krumm could not see.

"It's a white-sided roller," said Oblina, returning his eyes to him.

"Them's good eating," Krumm said, pleased.

"Hey! I think I've got something!" Ickis cried suddenly.

Oblina and Krumm rushed to his side.

"It's big," the little monster said. "We're talking major furniture."

Suddenly Ickis's stomach rumbled.

Politely, he covered his mouth as he burped.

"Wow!" said Krumm. "You're smokin'!"

"You really are," said Oblina. "Ickis, there is smoke coming out of your mouth."

But Ickis was not paying attention to his friends.

Struggling with his fishing rod, he declared, "This is going to put me in the 'Dump of Fame'!"

At last Ickis reeled in his line to find a wiggling fish at the end of it.

"A fish!" he gasped, disappointed.

"Tough luck," said Krumm.

"You'll do better next time," Oblina offered encouragingly.

"I really thought I had something," said Ickis.

Disgusted, he tossed the fish back into the water.

Then he burped again—blasting a burst of hot smoke at Krumm.

"You might want to get that checked," said Krumm when the smoke from Ickis's burp had cleared.

Krumm's face was covered with soot.

"What for?" Ickis asked glumly. "It's probably just something I ate."

Oblina and Krumm exchanged glances.

"I never saw anyone burp soot before," Krumm muttered.

"Where there's smoke, there's fire," Oblina observed.

The young monsters fished until they grew weary.

Then they packed up the ripe, rank, and rotten riches of the evening and headed for home.

Against the moonlit sky, three silhou-ettes moved across the dump, then disappeared into the sewer, one by one.

After dining on tin can cutlets and putrid melon-rind pies, they settled down to sleep.

"'Night, all," Oblina whispered, crawling onto her comfy old car seat.

Krumm plunked his eyes into a glass of murky water.

"'Night, buddies," he said. He snuggled under a blanket of smelly old socks in his doorless microwave.

"'Night—" Ickis was just drowsing off when he burped again. The pile of soggy newspapers on which he slept ignited and turned to ashes.

Once more, Krumm and Oblina exchanged worried glances.

But Ickis just murmured, "Indigestion. Excuse me, please," and fell asleep.

The next morning the three friends and their fellow students were taking a test.

The Gromble, the Academy's headmaster, paced before his class.

His black-gloved claws were clamped behind his broad back.

Oblina, the first monster to finish, set down her pencil.

Beside her, both Ickis and Krumm were still hard at work.

Mindlessly chewing his eraser, Ickis was puzzling over the question on Methods and Materials for Humbling Humans.

Eyes in one hand, pencil in the other, Krumm was bent over his paper, writing feverishly.

The Gromble, his red shoes tapping impatiently on the puddled floor of the underground classroom, glanced at the timer.

He saw that time had almost run out.

"Time!" the Gromble shouted, tapping the hourglass so that a final bit of banana peel fell through.

Ickis kept writing.

"Time, Master Ickis!!" The Gromble's voice rose to a deafening roar.

Heads snapped up, papers fluttered, and Ickis slammed down his pencil and grinned.

"Ickis," said the Gromble with a silky smile, "since you seem so eager to continue working, perhaps you will collect the tests and bring them to me."

"Of course, Your Scariness," Ickis cried, leaping to his feet.

"Thank you. Thank you. Thank you," he said, picking up exam papers.

When he had collected them all,

Ickis brought the large stack of tests to the Gromble.

"Here you go, sir—" he began.

A burp interrupted his sentence.

A blast of fire flew from his mouth and turned the papers to a pile of ash. Ickis trickled the ashes through his fingers into the waiting claws of the Gromble.

"Er . . . they're all there," Ickis said with a frightened grin. The Gromble stared in horror at the pile of ashes in his hand.

"Oblina," the Gromble called sweetly. "Would you watch the class?"

Then the headmaster turned to Ickis and roared, "Ickis! Come with me!"

With a scrape of red pumps on slimy sewer stones, the Gromble turned abruptly and marched Ickis out the door.

Zimbo, the Gromble's winged assistant, soared out of the classroom to spy on his master and poor Ickis.

He followed them through leaky

narrow tunnels and foul-smelling halls.

Then he saw the Gromble and Ickis enter the office of the school doctor.

Zimbo pressed his ear against the shut door.

The doctor, a small monster with a large reflector strapped to his ferocious head, stood on a stool in front of Ickis.

"Say 'ahhh,'" he said, holding a tongue depressor in Ickis's ear.

"Ahhh," Ickis said.

"Did you hear that?" the doctor demanded.

"Yes." Ickis nodded his head.

"Well, he can hear," the doctor told the Gromble.

Then the doctor grabbed Ickis's large ears and began to twirl the startled young monster over his head.

"Are you dizzy?" he asked, setting Ickis down.

"Uh . . . er . . . yeah," Ickis replied,

swaying wildly, trying to regain his balance.

"Good," said the doctor. "You should be."

Suddenly Ickis burped—burning the ends of the doctor's wispy hair and blackening his face with soot.

"I know! Let's take a look at that stomach," the doctor decided, wheeling an X-ray machine in front of Ickis.

Hair still smoking, the doctor clicked on the X-ray machine and gasped.

The inside of Ickis's stomach looked like a little garbage dump, but that was to be expected.

What troubled the doctor was the bright red light glowing in the center of that trash-filled stomach.

"Oh my," he cried, "he's going to blow!"

The Gromble watched the doctor run for cover.

Ickis burped again—this time the

flames that leaped from his mouth zapped the X-ray machine. It exploded in a shower of sparks!

"What is it?" the worried Gromble roared.

"There's only one way to find out," the doctor replied. "I'm going in!"

He climbed up on the stool and ordered Ickis to open wide.

He peered inside Ickis's mouth.

"Aha!" he cried, and peered in deeper.

"Oh-ho!" he shouted, and wriggled down into Ickis's stomach.

The sounds of tin cans clattering and bottles sloshing drew Zimbo closer to the door.

"Yow! Ooo! Ah! Eeeeee! Ah!" the doctor screeched, pulling his head and arm out of Ickis's mouth.

The doctor's stethoscope was gone, and his thumb was on fire.

He blew it out.

"This is bad," he told the Gromble.

"Bad . . . really bad . . . bad, bad, bad . . ."

"What are you saying?" Ickis asked.

"That this is not good," said the doctor. "You're spontaneously combustible."

Ickis scratched his head.

"Spin-top-iously cus-tard-able?" he said.

"Spontaneously combustible," the doctor corrected. "The good news is, it only lasts a week. The bad news is that the next burp could be your last."

Outside the door, Zimbo gasped.

"At any moment, son," the doctor said, "you could explode!"

"Could you be more specific?" Ickis asked.

"KA-BOOM!" the doctor said.

"Ka-Boom?!" Zimbo hissed, his spiky green hair standing more on end than ever.

"Ka-Boom," he murmured again, then flapped away.

"What do you mean . . . 'KA-BOOM!'?" Oblina wanted to know several hours later.

She and Krumm had returned to their dormitory to find Ickis covering the room in plastic.

"For the next seven days," he explained to his concerned friends, "I'm a disaster waiting to happen."

"And what happens after seven days?" asked Krumm.

"If I'm still here," a sad, dejected Ickis said, "we can take the plastic off the furniture."

*   *   *

"KA-BOOM!!" Zimbo flapped above the lunchroom table where Ickis's other classmates were cleaning their plates of runny mops with scummy sauce and sponges.

"That's what the doctor said," Zimbo whispered into one of Cower's six pitted pink ears.

A strand of greasy mop trailing from his open mouth, Cower looked horrified.

He leaned over to Galooth, who was already purple in the face, and whispered the shocking news about Ickis.

Sitting on the other side of Galooth, Bappy's sharp blue antennae had already picked up the information.

Ufwapo, chugging a can of canola oil, heard the whispers and, stunned, spit out a thick stream of yellow goo.

"Ka-Boom?!" they all whispered.

Meanwhile, Ickis slumped dejected in his dark room.

On his head was a rusty old sandbox pail, its metal handle tucked under his chin.

"Ickis, I know this is serious," Oblina said, "but you cannot spend the week sitting here in the dorm."

Ickis sighed and adjusted his safety helmet.

"Is there some place custardable monsters are supposed to sit?" he asked Oblina glumly.

"Combustible," she gently corrected him.

Krumm put a hairy arm around Ickis's shoulder, the eye in his hand watching his sad friend with concern.

"Come on, you look like the same old Ickis to me," Krumm said, helping Ickis to his feet and walking him toward the door.

"Except for that silly pail on your head," Krumm added.

Ickis gave Krumm an embarrassed smile and removed the rusty helmet.

Oblina joined them as they made their way through the sewer back to class.

"Well said, Krumm," remarked Oblina, swaying her slender body around a sticky old gallon drum in their path. "You are the same old Ickis; you have not changed. And nobody will change the way they treat you."

Wedged lovingly between his friends, Ickis shyly entered the Academy classroom.

A ripple of nervousness shuddered through the students already seated.

Ickis offered his classmates an enormous smile.

After an awkward moment, two of them grinned back tensely.

Ickis turned gratefully toward the brave pair—and burped.

Temporarily blinded by smoke, Ickis

heard a loud whoosh of air.

When the smoke cleared, the entire class, everyone except Krumm and Oblina, was on the other side of the room.

Shivering and shaking, they squeezed together on top of one another, as far away from Ickis as they could get.

"He's going to blow," someone whispered, sounding scared.

Ickis's shoulders sagged sadly, and his eyes welled unexpectedly with tears.

Nobody moved.

A dozen of the finest, scariest monsters sat trembling at the sight of Ickis—until they heard the familiar clicking sounds of the Gromble's shoes.

All heads spun toward the Academy's ferocious headmaster.

"Everybody back in your seats!" the Gromble ordered.

Slowly, reluctantly, Ickis's classmates

returned to their assigned seats.

"Now, you'll be pleased to know that we're not going to discuss your miserable attempts at scaring during the last week," the Gromble announced.

It was hard for Krumm to keep from shouting, *Yes!*

Oblina already had her pencil poised.

Ickis's red ears turned redder. His tummy churned. He tried his very best to pay attention to the lecture.

Most of the other monsters, however, sat in quaking silence, stealing terrified glances at Ickis whenever the Gromble's back was turned.

"Instead, I think you could all use a quick lesson in history," the Gromble continued. He stepped over to a set of large boards resting on an easel made of soiled and splintered pool cues.

On the first large board was the portrait of a shaggy, large, ugly monster with pointy teeth and horns.

The Gromble tapped the portrait with the soup bone he used as a pointer.

"Does anyone know who that is?" he asked.

Snav, a smaller version of the monster on the board, raised his hand.

"Yes, Snav?" the Gromble said.

"That's my great-uncle Sniv," Snav replied.

The Gromble waited, but Snav, grinning proudly, had nothing more to say.

"And does anyone know what he did for monsters everywhere?" the Gromble prompted.

Snav's hand shot up again.

It was rare for Snav to know an answer, and he was very excited.

"Yes, Snav?" the Gromble asked.

"He was my great-uncle!" Snav answered again.

For a moment, the Gromble gazed

at Snav with pity, then he glared around the room again.

"Can anyone tell us why he was important to *all* of us?" he roared.

"Being my great-uncle wasn't enough?" Snav whispered to the wide-eyed monster sitting next to him.

Again, his hairy little hand shot up.

The Gromble ignored him and scanned the room for someone else.

Oblina gave Snav an encouraging smile and, reluctantly, raised her hand.

"Ahhhh, Oblina." The Gromble's face brightened.

"He was the greatest philosopher in modern monster history," Oblina recited. "It was the great Sniv who said, 'I scare, therefore, I am.'"

"Thank you, Oblina," the Gromble said, pleased.

He removed the picture of Snav's great-uncle.

Beneath it was a portrait of a distinguished blue monster who looked very much like the Gromble himself.

"And here's Kladiac," the Gromble crooned with a flourish of his soup bone. "Kladiac, the Mighty, who pioneered the Great Northern Sewer System.

"He was uncommonly handsome," the Gromble added, showing his own powerful profile to the class.

With a frightening, satisfied smile, he tossed aside the picture of Kladiac.

The last board on the easel showed a tall, thin, many-armed monster who was striped like Oblina.

"Ooooh," the whole class murmured, for this handsome monster was very popular.

"Yes, this is the beloved Pupulula," the Gromble said, "whose singing and mediocre talents entertained thousands of monsters during . . . the 'Era of Disbelief.'"

Snav raised his hand once more.

The Gromble glared at him, then gently said, "Yes, Snav, that first one was your great-uncle."

Snav nodded happily and put down his hand.

"Ickis?" said the Gromble. "Can you guess what all these monsters had in common?"

Ickis did not know.

"Each of them was," the Gromble emphasized, *spontaneously com-bust-ible.*"

The chattering of snaggled monster teeth echoed through the classroom.

"And . . . er . . . none of them blew up?" Ickis asked hopefully.

"It doesn't matter at all IF THEY BLEW UP OR NOT," the Gromble shouted, pounding the easel with his pointer.

The whoosh of monsters sliding and scurrying across the benches reached his ears.

"What matters is—combustible or not," roared the Gromble, whirling angrily toward the class, "they were each an important part of our monster world!"

Ickis, Oblina, and Krumm sat alone on one side of the lecture hall.

A cluster of quivering monsters huddled on the other side.

"Nobody ever became combustible by sitting next to a combustible someone!" he concluded. "NOW, BACK TO YOUR SEATS!"

Nervously, Ickis's classmates slid back across the benches.

Ickis smiled back at them.

Then he burped.

A burst of smoke escaped his lips.

The class tore back to the far side of the room.

Ickis, Krumm, and Oblina had to hold on to their seats to avoid being swept along by the rush of air that followed their anxious classmates.

"It's not your fault, Ickis," Oblina said, trying to comfort her friend.

"Yeah. They're just jealous," Krumm sneered. "I bet they wish they could burp and burn like you."

Ickis didn't think so.

"Excuse me, Your Great Grombleness." He raised his hand. "May I please be excused?"

With a nod of his blue-winged head, the Gromble said, "Go."

When Krumm and Oblina returned
to the dormitory, Ickis was nowhere to
be seen.

Krumm scanned the room.

Lying beside his slightly crushed
microwave was the delicious tire he'd
caught fishing.

Turned upside down on Ickis's lumpy
bed was a rusty, dented metal bowl with
holes in it.

Dung beetles skittered over Oblina's
favorite chair.

But no Ickis.

Oblina moved swiftly past Krumm.

She went directly to Ickis's bed
and lifted the metal bowl.

"You must not take things so per-
sonally, Ickie," she said to the young
monster huddled beneath it.

Ickis sighed a wisp of smoke and
peered up at Oblina. "But nobody wants
to be my friend anymore," he said.

"I'm your buddy, buddy," Krumm
pointed out. "Hey, come on, let's go
have some supper."

"I don't think so," said Ickis.

"You will feel better with something
in your tummy," Oblina agreed.

"I already have something in my
tummy!" Ickis replied snappishly. "It's
glowing and growing, and it's going to
EXPLODE!"

"Not necessarily," Oblina reminded
him. "Now, let us go and get a little
snack before bedtime. There is a tempting,
terrible smell coming from the dining
sewer."

"And lots of noise, too," said Krumm.

"Sounds like everyone's having a lot of fun in there."

"Well . . ." said Ickis skeptically. "Okay."

All conversation stopped the moment the trio entered the noisy hall.

A dozen startled monster faces swung toward the door.

Eyes widened with fear.

"Be brave," Oblina whispered.

With all the courage he could muster, Ickis approached the table where Galooth and Bappy, a moment before, had been happily gobbling crusty bug shells and snails.

"Excuse me," Ickis said with a friendly smile, "is that seat taken?"

The entire table emptied at once.

"No," Bappy called back from across the room.

Ickis's shoulders slumped in defeat.

"It's okay. I'm really not very

hungry," he announced.

Then, with a brave smile and a forced wave, he left the dining hall.

Oblina and Krumm exchanged a grave look.

Oblina turned to glare at the quaking monsters cowering in a cobwebbed corner of the room.

Hands on her hips, she studied one face after another.

"Are we not monsters?!" she wanted to demand.

But the ugly faces she saw staring back at her seemed very small and very frightened.

"Forget about what they think," she told Ickis later. "They are like that because they are young—they do not understand."

Ickis was already in bed.

"What about you?" he asked Oblina,

peering out from under the big, rusty bowl.

"I am wise beyond my years," she said, and yawned sleepily.

Krumm was in bed, too, eyeing the heaping tray of food they'd brought back for Ickis.

They had filled it with oozing squashed tennis balls, a soothing shower curtain soup, and rusted potato peelers.

But Ickis had refused to eat a bite.

Reaching out from under his smelly old blanket, Krumm selected a wet tennis ball from the tray.

Oblina wriggled into her night sock and settled into the car seat.

"Do take that ridiculous thing off your back, Ickis," she urged, pointing at the foul bowl.

"It's to protect you and Krumm," he explained, "in case I blow in the middle of the night."

One fiery burp
turned papers to ash.

The Gromble listened to the rumors.

"Krumm! Krumm! You came back!" One by one, every monster in the Academy appeared.

"We're perfectly safe, I'm sure," she said. "Don't you agree, Krumm?"

"Hmmumph," said Krumm, biting into the chewy tennis ball.

"You do not have to make yourself uncomfortable on our account," Oblina said as she shut off the light.

"Good night, guys," said Ickis.

Krumm swallowed the ball with a gulp.

"Good night, Oblina," he called, dropping his eyes into the glass of water beside his bed. "Good night, Ickis."

The dormitory was black and still.

"If I blow up in the middle of the night," Ickis called into the darkness, "I'll try not to wake you."

"Go to sleep, Ickis. We will see you in the morning," said Oblina.

Ickis shut his eyes at last.

The night silence was suddenly broken
by a pounding on the dormitory door.

Oblina flicked on the light.

Ickis peeked out from under his bowl.

"Come in," he called.

A large, hairy monster, wearing a
frozen smile, entered the room.

"Horvak!" Ickis and Oblina cried,
delighted.

The nervously grinning grown-up
monster raised his arms in greeting.

An eye-watering stench filled the room.

"Dad!" Krumm called, leaping out of
bed in a flash.

Ickis and Oblina watched as Krumm
and Horvak kicked each other in greeting.

"Hi there, Oblina. Hello, Ickis, how's your dad?" Horvak asked as though he were in a great hurry.

"Er—," said Ickis.

"Great to hear it," Horvak hollered before Ickis could even answer. "Pack your bag, Krumm."

Ickis and Oblina looked at each other.

Horvak was talking unusually fast, even for him.

And the smile he had plastered on his face looked far more grim than glad.

Horvak rushed to Krumm's closet and began tossing things into his son's suitcase.

"What's going on, Dad?" Krumm asked.

"Oh, you know. Time to harvest the mold," Horvak said very quickly. "I need you at home."

"Krumm?" Ickis asked, confused. "Didn't you say your dad harvested the mold last week?"

Horvak heard the question and hurried across the room.

"That's what I thought, too," he answered, taking Krumm's arm abruptly and pulling him toward the door. "But there it is, still in the fields. Come on, Krumm, let's hit the sewer."

"Wow!" Krumm was really excited. "The mold harvest is great. Ickis, you want to come along?"

Before Ickis could say a word, Horvak shook his big head no.

"No, no, no. Whoa!" Krumm's father said. "Ickis? Ickis? No, Ickis, doesn't want to come. Hi there, Ickis, how's your dad?"

This time, Ickis didn't even try to answer.

He picked up a soggy paper bag and quickly blew it up.

With a clap of his hand, he exploded it. *Ka-Boom!*

Oblina immediately shut her eyes tightly, then slowly opened them to see if Ickis was all right.

What she saw was Horvak shaking with fear.

His head was buried inside Krumm's microwave.

Ickis saw him, too.

Horvak climbed out from inside the microwave and glared at Ickis. He grabbed Krumm.

"Come on, son. Let's get out of here," he said, pushing him to the door.

"Bye, buddy." Krumm waved to Ickis, then disappeared.

The door slammed shut behind him.

Ickis stared at it blankly.

Oblina cleared her throat, trying to get his attention.

But Ickis continued to stare straight ahead.

"Krumm did not want to leave," she declared.

Ickis burped, and squinted absently through the smoke.

"I am sure of it, Ickis," Oblina said.

"What does it matter?" Ickis asked.

He threw down the burst bag and looked around.

"Your parents will be next," he said, picking through a pile of rubbish to find the little banana peel basket Krumm had given him long ago.

Ickis placed a few of his personal belongings in the basket.

He packed a stained bit of cloth on which Oblina had written a poem for him.

He packed a jelly jar full of insects Krumm had caught for his birthday.

Finally, he packed a pair of half-eaten plyers, his favorite marble, and one of the cold tennis balls left over from dinner.

"And then everybody's mom and dad will come," he said, "and pull them out of school."

Clutching the banana peel basket, Ickis walked out into the hallway.

Oblina followed after him. "That is ridiculous, Ickis," she said. "No one is going to leave the Academy because of you."

She stopped and gasped.

The long, dark dormitory hall was crowded with lumbering monster parents dragging trunks and boxes out of their children's rooms.

"What are you doing?" Ickis demanded furiously. "Everybody packing your bags?"

Snav's shaggy horned head and Cower's six huge ears popped out of their rooms to stare at him.

Their parents quickly pushed them back inside.

Bappy's alarmed blue face appeared in the corridor.

"Get back in there!" his father commanded, thick antennae waving above his head like fists.

"You trying to get away from me before I blow you up?" Ickis hollered.

Even parents were running for cover now, ducking into their children's rooms or scrambling for the nearest sewer pipe.

"Well, I've got news for you," Ickis screamed louder than ever. "You can stay here—because I'm going!"

"Ickis, don't . . ." Oblina called.

But it was too late.

Ickis wrenched open the sewer door and stepped out into the night.

With a loud metallic clang, the door slammed shut behind him.

Immediately the Gromble insisted that all students gather at once in the classroom.

Looking angrier than they'd ever seen him, the Gromble paced gravely before them.

He slapped his black-gloved palm with his soup bone pointer.

His full red lips were pulled down at the corners in a fierce frown.

When the last of the sleepy monsters settled into their seats, the Gromble turned on them furiously.

"I suppose you all know that Ickis is gone," he began in a frighteningly silky voice.

The young monsters nodded nervously, but could not meet the Gromble's fierce glare.

"And you all knew that Ickis was combustible?" he asked.

They nodded again, sleepily.

"But do any of you," the Gromble demanded, "know what that means?!"

He scanned their faces.

His scowling eyes fell on Cower.

Cower's pink face peered slowly around the room.

Finally, he raised one clawed hand and said, "Sir? Er . . . exalted Scare-master? Ickis was going to explode!"

Turning to Galooth for help, Cower added, "Wasn't he?"

Galooth dipped his small purple head and tried to look away.

"Come on, Galooth. Wasn't he going to explode?" Cower asked again.

Galooth found his courage and cleared his throat.

"He was going to go Ka-Boom at any moment," he agreed, "in a great big ball of fire."

Now Bappy joined in.

"A ball of fire so big that it could blow up the whole school!" he said.

Ufwapo turned his hairy brown head and looked suspiciously at Bappy.

"You told me," he complained gruffly, "that Ickis could blow up the whole dump."

The Gromble closed his eyes, and shook his great green head in disbelief. "Who told you that?" he roared.

Ufwapo pointed to Bappy, whose tight blue face blushed nearly black.

Bappy swung his antennaed head toward Galooth, who grinned tensely.

Galooth's huge purple ears nearly swatted Cower's frightened pink face.

"He did," Cower said, pointing to Zimbo.

Zimbo smiled sheepishly at the Gromble.

"I believed," he began in his wheedling, whiny way, "that the free exchange of information was the key to better understanding."

The Gromble's stare turned even more icy.

"In other words," Zimbo tried again, "I thought it was important to inform the student body of dear Ickis's misfortune."

The Gromble's face clouded dangerously.

With a shrug of his bee-striped body, Zimbo said, "Perhaps I was misinformed."

"You've all been MISINFORMED," the Gromble raged. "I told you he wasn't a danger to any of you."

Zimbo nodded quickly. "That's right. Exactly. Oh, isn't he bright."

"But you listened to rumors!" The Gromble tugged his head wings in frustration.

A new flurry of fear swept the sleepy monsters.

Few had ever seen the Gromble so disturbed.

He stood before them, his red-clad toes tapping impatiently, his soup bone pounding his palm.

"Do you know what we call someone who is scared of something he doesn't understand?" he asked very, very quietly.

Only Oblina raised her hand.

The Gromble nodded in her direction. "Oblina?"

"Human," she said. "Someone who is scared of something he does not understand is how the *Monster Manual* describes humans."

"So," the Gromble said, satisfied, "is that what you want to act like? A bunch of HUMANS?"

"No way!"

"Eeeww!"

"Never!"

The monsters shook their heads.

A sadder but wiser Zimbo joined them.

Even Snorch began to shake his head— which was a big mistake since Zimbo was standing on it.

To steady himself, Zimbo dug his sharp claws more deeply into Snorch's scalp.

"Yikes!" Snorch hollered.

"Exactly," said the Gromble. "We cannot afford to sink so low!"

A cold rain lashed the dump.

Followed by a scruffy, wet rat, Ickis wandered between rusting car parts and bloated plastic bags seeking shelter.

A crack of lightning lit the muddy night.

Clutching his small basket against him, Ickis saw the dark silhouette of a bridge up ahead.

He was in no hurry, however.

He didn't care whether he caught a cold or not.

Everyone was afraid of him.

Even grown-up monsters had hurried out of his way.

What difference would a cold make to him now?

So he'd sneeze smoke.

So he'd cough flames.

So what?!

Feet splashing through deepening puddles, Ickis continued on at a slow and steady pace.

Eager to find a dry place, the rat now scampered ahead of him.

Ickis recalled how startled Krumm had been at the sound of the paper bag popping.

Oblina had flinched, too.

Even his best friends were frightened of him.

With a heavy heart and a rumbling tummy, Ickis followed the rat.

By the time they reached the bridge, he was soaked.

Ickis ducked down under the dank, sour-smelling walls of the bridge and prepared to settle in for the night.

It was colder than he'd thought it would be.

What he needed was a campfire.

There was a pile of dry newspapers nearby, but there were no matches to be found.

Ickis stared at the papers and scratched his head.

Then he burped—and a tiny spark exploded from his mouth, lighting one edge of the paper.

Soon Ickis had a roaring fire going.

He found a shoe, a wormy jar of peanut butter, and even a sticky, tattered old sweater he could use as a blanket.

Sitting beside the campfire, Ickis untied the shoe and tasted the thick leather lace.

The rat looked up at him hungrily.

"Here you go, buddy," Ickis said,

tearing the frayed lace and offering half
to the rat.

The rat drew closer.

Ickis sneezed.

A burst of smoke and flames whooshed
out of his mouth.

The rat's wide eyes stared out of a
soot-blackened face.

"Excuse me," Ickis said.

But the rat scurried away.

"Yeah, run from me," Ickis called
weakly after his former friend.
"Everybody else does. And you know
what?"

He tossed the shoe aside and opened
his sopping-wet banana peel basket.

"I don't care," he continued, digging
through his mementos.

He found the stained piece of material
on which Oblina had written her poem.

"I don't need friends who won't
stand by me," he said, rubbing his

cheek with the precious filthy fabric.

"So I blow up. If they want to live their lives scared of something that's not even happening to them," Ickis said, folding the poem back into the basket, "then, you know what? They've got a bigger problem than I do."

He stood boldly.

"Me?" he said, shoulders back, chin defiantly raised. "I'll face this alone. I'm not scared."

Somewhere a truck backfired.

"HELP!" Ickis leaped into the air, screaming.

He scrambled up the stone wall under the bridge and gripped on to it fearfully.

The truck rumbled by overhead, backfiring once more.

Ickis squeezed shut his eyes and, with one hand, clutched his tummy, expecting to explode.

As the truck moved off into the

distance, Ickis climbed carefully down.

He was breathing heavily.

He was shaking with fear.

"Go ahead, Life," he shouted at the top of his lungs. "Toy with me. Play your cruel jokes. I don't care."

Somewhere in the rainy night, Krumm heard his friend shouting.

He followed Ickis's voice across the dump to the bridge.

Krumm looked under the run-down old bridge.

At the opposite end, Ickis was staring skyward and shaking his fist at the rain.

"I don't care about anything," Ickis hollered.

Krumm walked quietly up beside him and looked at the sky, trying to figure out who Ickis was talking to.

He couldn't see anyone.

So he shrugged and waited until Ickis was done.

"I don't care about anyone," Ickis shouted.

Then he was silent.

"Hi, Ickis," Krumm said.

"Yikes!" Ickis clutched his heart.

When he recognized his old friend, his anger disappeared at once.

"Krumm?" he said, not quite believing it.

Krumm grinned his rotten-toothed grin. "Beautiful night."

"Krumm! Krumm! You came back," Ickis exclaimed joyously. He ran to give his friend a hug.

"Sure," Krumm said, "the minute Oblina got word to me that you'd left. I'm sorry, Ickis."

"It's okay." Ickis lowered his head shyly.

"Naw, you're my friend," Krumm insisted. "I should have stuck beside you. As soon as I heard you ran away, I went back to the Academy. But no one was there."

"That's because," a raspy voice said, "we were all out looking for Ickis."

Ickis and Krumm turned to find Snav's horned head poking up from an old trash can.

"Snav?!"

Oblina's upside-down face came into view.

She was hanging by her feet from the top of the bridge.

"The Gromble made everyone see how they had been treating you, Ickie," she explained.

Oblina did a deft back flip and landed on her feet beside Krumm.

Now Ufwapo's drooling brown lips grinned at Ickis.

"Yeah, we couldn't sleep, anyway," he said, spotting and scooping up the rancid shoe.

One by one every young monster in the Academy appeared and moved cautiously toward Ickis.

"Sorry," said Cower, patting Ickis's back with a powerful claw.

"If we knew everything we wouldn't need school, would we?" Bappy asked, squeezing Ickis's hand.

"How're you feeling?" Galooth wanted to know.

Ickis started to sneeze.

Everyone took a tiny step back.

Except Ufwapo, who was wetly gnawing the rotten shoe.

"Ah . . . ah . . . CHOO!" Ickis sneezed.

"Er . . . sorry, Ufwapo," he quickly apologized to the surprised little brown monster, who was staring down at the ashes in his hand.

Everyone laughed.

Even Ufwapo.

And then they all walked Ickis back through the dump to the big sewer door.

Ickis was very tired.

Gratefully, he climbed into bed.

With a *clunk, clang, crash,* the rusted metal bowl rolled off his head. It hit the floor and rolled into a musty corner.

"Good night, guys," Ickis called out.

"Good night, Ickie," Oblina whispered from her car seat.

"'Night, Ickis," Krumm mumbled from his microwave.

"Good night, Ickis!" all the other little monsters sang out from their beds.

The whole class was crammed into Ickis's little dorm room.

Suddenly, Zimbo stuck his green spiked head out from behind Ickis's refrigerator.

"Yes, as they said—good night, Ickis."

9

"Don't worry, Ickis. We'll be with you," Oblina promised.

It was five days later.

Ickis had a slight cold and a second appointment with the school doctor.

The three friends splashed down the sewer toward the doctor's office.

"It's been a week," Krumm pointed out. "If you haven't gone Ka-Boom yet, you're cured, right?"

"Right," Ickis said, but he couldn't help worrying.

Oblina noticed.

"No matter what happens, Ickis, you are not alone."

"Good luck, Ickis," Snav called down the long corridor.

"You'll be fine," Bappy declared.

"If anything goes wrong, can I have your marble?" Ufwapo hollered.

"That is so negative!" Cower glared at his friend.

Ufwapo looked hurt. "I meant . . . just until Ickis comes back," he explained.

In the infirmary, Ickis waited between Oblina and Krumm as the doctor fooled around with the dials of the X-ray machine.

Pulling it in front of Ickis, he switched it on.

"Whoa!" the doctor said.

"What?" asked Ickis.

"It's been seven days. He should be fine," said Oblina.

"What do you mean, 'Whoa'?" Krumm wanted to know.

The doctor bit his blue lips with his

sharp little teeth and studied Ickis's X ray.

Puzzled, he shook his head. "There it is!" he cried suddenly.

The doctor slid the X-ray machine to one side.

"Open your mouth," he ordered Ickis.

Oblina and Krumm waited nervously nearby.

Ickis opened his mouth.

The doctor stuck his hand down into Ickis's throat.

"Ugh, whugh, wha?" Ickis said as the doctor fished around inside of him.

"Aha!" the doctor said, pulling his stethoscope out of Ickis's mouth.

"I've been looking for this for a week!" he announced.

The doctor put his stethoscope back around his neck.

Ickis, Krumm, and Oblina watched and waited for the doctor to tell Ickis whether everything was all right or not.

"Are you still here?" asked the doctor after a moment.

"Well, I wanted to know if I still have to worry about blowing up," Ickis said.

"Blowing up?" The doctor shook his head. "No—you're healthy as the day you were born. In fact, healthy monsters like you have no business in my office."

"Yes!" Ickis shouted.

"Congratulations, Ickie!" Oblina cheered.

"Way to go, buddy!" Krumm grinned and threw his arms in the air.

A rat munching cheese in the corner keeled over from the fumes.

"Go on, clear out," said the doctor. "All of you."

With a monstrous whoop, they ran for the door and slammed it loudly behind them.

"Yea! Hooray! You're fine again!"

"I'm okay." Ickis nodded.

"Let's go tell everybody," said Oblina. As they hurried along the steamy sewer, doors opened, monsters cheered.

"You're all better!" Bappy said happily.

"No more Ka-Boom!" Snav's pointy-toothed grin spread from ear to shaggy ear.

"Can I just *borrow* your marble?" Ufwapo asked.

"Sure," Ickis said. "No problem, pal."

"Excuse me," Oblina interrupted. "How did everyone find out about Ickis so quickly?"

All heads whirled toward Zimbo, who was perched, as usual, on Snorch's head.

"Proud to be the bearer of good tidings," Zimbo crooned smugly.

"Let's celebrate!" Galooth suggested.

"Party time!" Cower called.

"I'll roast the cans and galoshes. Who's got the gravy?" another monster volunteered.

Everyone scurried through the sewer pipes to prepare for Ickis's party.

All except Oblina, Krumm, and Ickis.

"I've got a better idea," Ickis said when they were alone.

A sly smile spread across his red face.

"I know that look," Oblina remarked.

"It's about hooks and lines and sinkers," Krumm guessed.

"It is about fishing poles," said Oblina, whipping herself around like a striped pole with a gallon drum of glop at the end of it.

"Yeah!" Ickis said. "LET'S GO FISHING!"

The sun was setting.

The old bridge was damp and slippery, crawling with slimy creatures.

Bats hanging from the ceiling were just beginning to stir.

The clogged river flowed lazily by.

Rotting garbage and broken furniture, metal files and punctured tires bobbed in the current.

And three monster friends sat at the foul river's edge, fishing contentedly in the cool, red twilight.